...aphic design at the University
...A in Illustration at Manchester
...cclaimed picture books for
... *Home* (with Mary Hoffman),
...y Grindley), *Home Now*
...*ory* (with Genevieve Moore)
...iz Weir). *Star Girl* is the first
...itten and illustrated for
...oks. She lives in London.

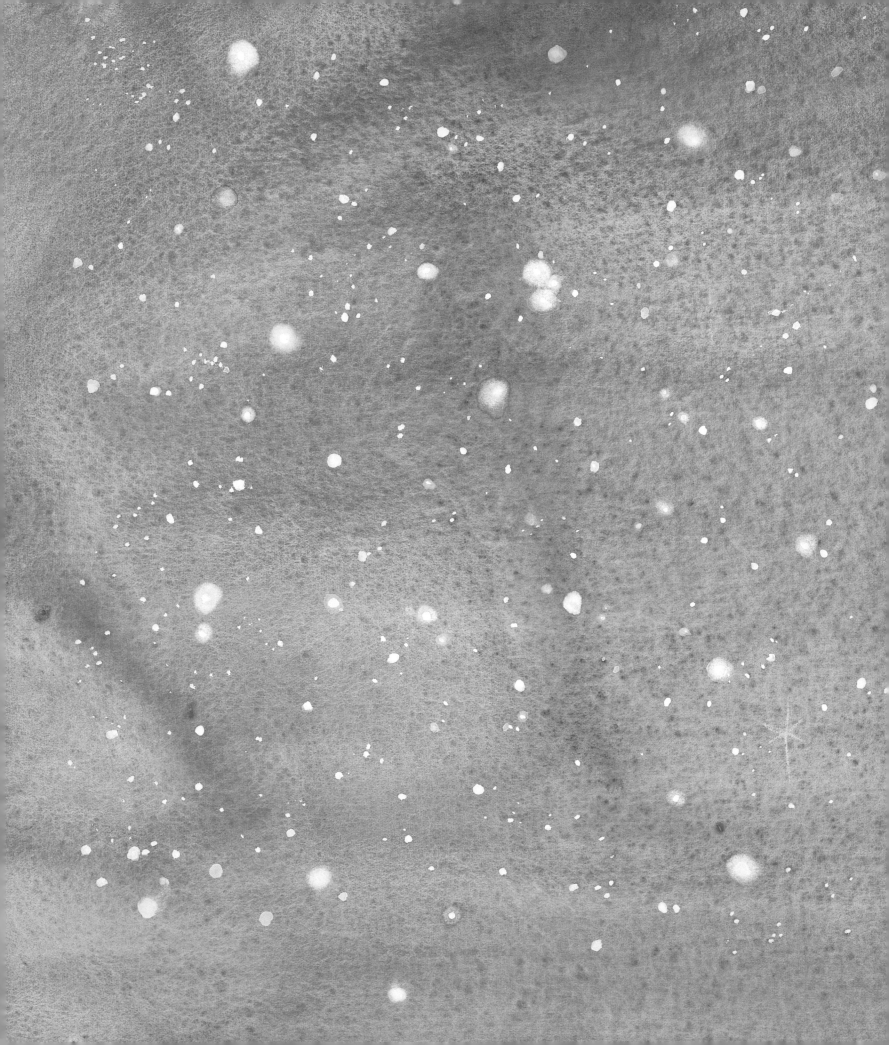

For Lara

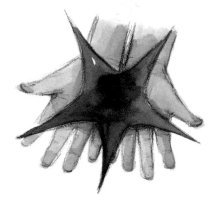

JANETTA OTTER-BARRY BOOKS

Text and illustrations copyright © Karin Littlewood 2013
The right of Karin Littlewood to be identified as the Author and Illustrator of this Work
has been asserted by her in accordance with the Copyright, Designs and Patents Act, 1988 (United Kingdom).
First published in Great Britain and in the USA in 2013 by
Frances Lincoln Children's Books,
74-77 White Lion Street, Islington N1 9PF
www.franceslincoln.com

First published in paperback in Great Britain in 2014 and in the USA in 2015

A CIP catalogue record for this book is available from the British Library.

ISBN 978-1-84780-521-8

Printed in China

1 3 5 7 9 8 6 4 2

STAR GIRL

Karin Littlewood

F

FRANCES LINCOLN
CHILDREN'S BOOKS

Gracie had a star.
Every night it shone for her
outside her bedroom window.
"You're my special star," she whispered.

But each morning the star had gone.

"I miss you," Gracie said softly as she searched the sky. "I wish you were here with me all the time."

So one very quiet night, Gracie
crept into the forest and climbed
to the top of the tallest tree.
   She reached far into the twinkling
sky and gently caught hold of her
beautiful shining star.

But when she got back home and took the star
from her pocket it didn't shine so brightly.
Grace rubbed it and rubbed it to make it shine,
but nothing happened.

"You must be tired, just like me," she yawned.

In the morning Gracie filled her room
with all her things that shimmered
and spangled, glistened and glowed.

She put on her starry dress and shiny shoes
and danced for her star…
but nothing happened, not even a twinkle.

Gracie couldn't wait until the evening
when her star would shine again,
just as it always did.
    When twilight came she carried her star
to the top of the hill. Far away, hundreds
of stars began to glitter.

All except one. . .

Look! There were fireworks in the town below.
The night sky sang with colours.
Gracie held her little star high.
  "Please shine for me!" she begged.

"Are you lonely?" asked Gracie.
But the star couldn't answer.

So she took it to the place where the fireflies
flittered and the glow worms glowed.
But her little star just swayed in the breeze.

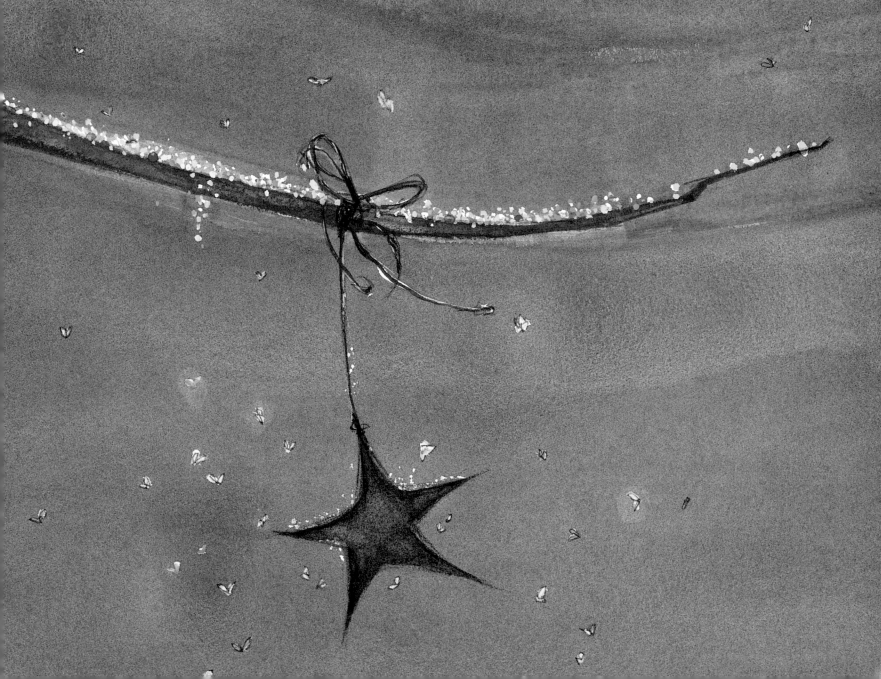

The next day Gracie ran down to the sea.
  "You need some friends... and I know
just where to find them!"
  She put her star in the rock-pools amongst
the starfish. But it just lay there sadly.

There was one special place where Gracie
knew her star would feel at home.
　　When night fell, she took her little boat
and bobbed out to sea. She slipped the star
into the water and watched with excitement
as the moon and the stars danced
on the waves.

And then she thought she saw
a little glimmer…
a tiniest twinkle…
the smallest spark….

Gracie held her star tightly as droplets
of water fell from it like diamonds.

She looked and looked at her star.
It lay in her hands, cold and dull
and grey. Nothing had changed!
Gracie knew then that her star
would never shine for her again.

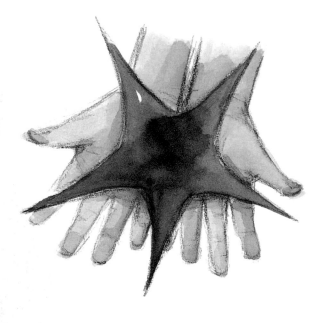

The night wind was blowing
and the moon hung low and silver.
It seemed as though the world
was filled with all the stars
that had ever been.

"You belong in the night sky,
not with me," Gracie cried.
She gently kissed her beautiful
star goodbye, and let it go.

Then, more than ever, Gracie needed her home too.
Soon, she was back in her own little bed.
Sadly she closed her eyes.
   But suddenly she felt something calling her.
She looked out of her window. . .

And there it was! Brilliant in the night sky,
one star shone brighter than ever before.
   It was her star, shining once again, just for Gracie.

MORE BEAUTIFUL PICTURE BOOKS ILLUSTRATED BY KARIN LITTLEWOOD
FROM FRANCES LINCOLN CHILDREN'S BOOKS

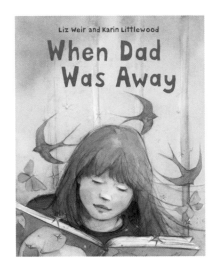

When Dad Was Away
Written by Liz Weir

Milly's dad has been sent to prison, and at first Milly feels angry and confused. But after a visit to Dad, and a Christmas party at the prison, in the spring comes the best surprise of all...

"A compassionate story, sensitively told and delicately illustrated" – *Early Years Educator*

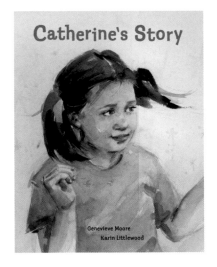

Catherine's Story
Written by Genevieve Moore

Catherine can clap her hands very quietly, she can walk smoothly in boots no one else can walk in, and she's a really good listener. This family picture book shows how all the things that make Catherine different also make her special.

"Superbly and sensitively written... the illustrations are an outstanding combination of warmth, love and understanding." – *Books for Keeps, 5-star review*

Frances Lincoln titles are available from all good bookshops.
You can also buy books and find out more about your favourite titles,
authors and illustrators on our website: www.franceslincoln.com